...Stop,
Thief!...

For my mom and dad, who are not only terrific parents but also great gardeners, doing their best to teach me how to grow carrots, berries, beans and cherries! — H.T.

Text © 2014 Heather Tekavec
Illustrations © 2014 Pierre Pratt

Kids Can Press acknowledges the financial support of the Government of Ontario, through the Ontario Media Development Corporation's Ontario Book Initiative; the Ontario Arts Council; the Canada Council for the Arts; and the Government of Canada, through the CBF, for our publishing activity.

Published in Canada by
Kids Can Press Ltd.
25 Dockside Drive
Toronto, ON M5A 0B5

Published in the U.S. by
Kids Can Press Ltd.
2250 Military Road
Tonawanda, NY 14150

www.kidscanpress.com

The artwork in this book was rendered in gouache on paper.
The text is set in Triplex.

Edited by Yasemin Uçar
Designed by Marie Bartholomew

This book is smyth sewn casebound.
Manufactured in Shenzhen, China, in 3/2014 through Asia Pacific Offset

CM 14 0 9 8 7 6 5 4 3 2 1

LIBRARY AND ARCHIVES CANADA CATALOGUING IN PUBLICATION

Tekavec, Heather, 1969–, author
    Stop, thief! / written by Heather Tekavec ; illustrated by Pierre Pratt.

ISBN 978-1-77138-012-6 (bound)

I. Pratt, Pierre, illustrator II. Title.

PS8589.E373S86 2014   jC813'.6   C2013-908217-4

Kids Can Press is a Corus™ Entertainment company

Stop, Thief!

WRITTEN BY

Heather Tekavec

ILLUSTRATED BY

Pierre Pratt

Kids Can Press

"Max," said the farmer to his dog one day, "can you catch a thief?" Max jumped up eagerly. He could catch anything!

"I don't know what he looks like," the farmer said, "but he's been stealing all the carrots, berries, beans and cherries. Go catch him before he eats my whole farm!"

So Max took a rope and ran to catch the thief.

He wasn't gone long before he heard a strange buzzing
sound. He followed the buzz to a small orange carrot.
On the orange carrot were some feathery green leaves.
On one of the leaves was a tiny blue bug.
And the bug was chewing the leaf!

Max leaped toward the bug. "Stop, thief!" he barked.
He tossed the rope over the bug. But the bug escaped.

A rabbit popped up behind the carrots.
"Are you ..." *nibble, nibble,* "... talking to me?"
the rabbit asked between mouthfuls of carrot.
"No," Max said. "I'm talking to the thief who's
eating all the carrots, berries, beans and cherries."

"A thief?" the rabbit asked. "Eating our carrots? How rude!"
The rabbit hopped and looked around. "But I don't see anyone,"
she said.

"He's hard to see," Max explained. "But he's here … and he's
very sly."

"In that case," she said, "you better go after him. Go, go, go!
I'll …" *nibble, nibble,* "… guard the carrots."

"Thanks," Max barked and ran off, while the rabbit stood guard.

In the berry patch, Max found the bug on a strawberry.
But when the bug saw him coming, it flew away.

"Stop, thief!" Max barked. He chased the bug up and down the rows of berries until he ran right into a round rump with a curly pink tail.

"Hello, Max," said the plump pig who was attached to the tail.
She lay on her back, sucking on a strawberry.

"Can't talk now," Max said. "I'm trying to catch the thief who's
eating all our carrots, berries, beans and cherries."

"Oh, dear!" the pig said. "That's not very nice." She swallowed and scowled and rolled onto her feet. "I'll watch the berries, while you go find him."

Max nodded and raced away to find the thief. Before long,
he heard buzzing in the beanfield. The bug was hiding
in the vines!

"Stop, thief!" Max barked. He chased it around in circles
until the bug zipped off through the field.

"Ma-a-a-x," a small voice bleated from behind the beans. "What are you doing?" The farmer's hungry little goat poked his head between the vines. A green bean fell out of his mouth.

"I'm trying to catch a thief," Max replied. "He's been eating all the carrots, berries, beans and cherries."

"That's gre-e-e-edy!" the goat bleated. "You go get him, Max. I'll take care of the beans."

So Max raced off again. And the goat began eating the beans as fast as he could so the thief couldn't get them.

"Just one more place to look," Max thought. He ran to the orchard and stopped to listen. Sure enough, Max could hear a faint buzzing in a nearby tree.

"Come down, thief!" Max barked.

"No thief up here," a voice squawked back. "Just me."

"And me."

"And me."

One by one, three black crows peeked out from the leaves.

The first one swallowed. "I'm Floyd," he said. "And these are my cousins, Roy and Orville."

"Pleased to meet you," Max said. "I'm trying to catch a thief. Have you seen him?"

"I don't think so," Orville said.

"Maybe," Roy said.

"What does he look like?" Floyd asked.

"He's small and blue and kind of buzzy," Max explained. "And he's stealing all the carrots, berries, beans and cherries."

"I think he went that way," Floyd said, pointing left.

"Then he went that way," Roy said, pointing right.

"And then he went that way," Orville added, pointing up.

Just then, the bug zipped right past their beaks!

"Go get him!" they all said together.

Max chased the bug out of the orchard, jumping and nipping as he ran. He chased it past the pond. He chased it through the field. He chased it around the barn, the house and the clothesline. Finally, the bug flew over the fence and disappeared.

"And don't ever come back!" Max barked after it.

When Max returned to the barn, the others were waiting for him. "Did you catch the thief?" they asked all at once.

"I scared him away for good," Max told them proudly.

"Yaaay!" the animals cheered. "Now the carrots, berries, beans and cherries will be safe!"

Max smiled and ran off to tell the farmer.

"We should have a party for Max," the rabbit suggested. "Let's get some food."

So the pig ran to get more berries, the goat went for beans, the rabbit brought carrots and the crows picked the last of the cherries.

The animals stared at the big pile of food.

"I sure hope Max hurries," the pig said.

The rabbit sniffed the carrots.

"What if the thief comes back," asked the goat, "and tries to steal all this good food?"

"We should hide it," the crows said, and all the animals agreed.

So the animals worked as fast as they could until all the carrots, berries, beans and cherries were safely hidden …

... where the thief could never find them!

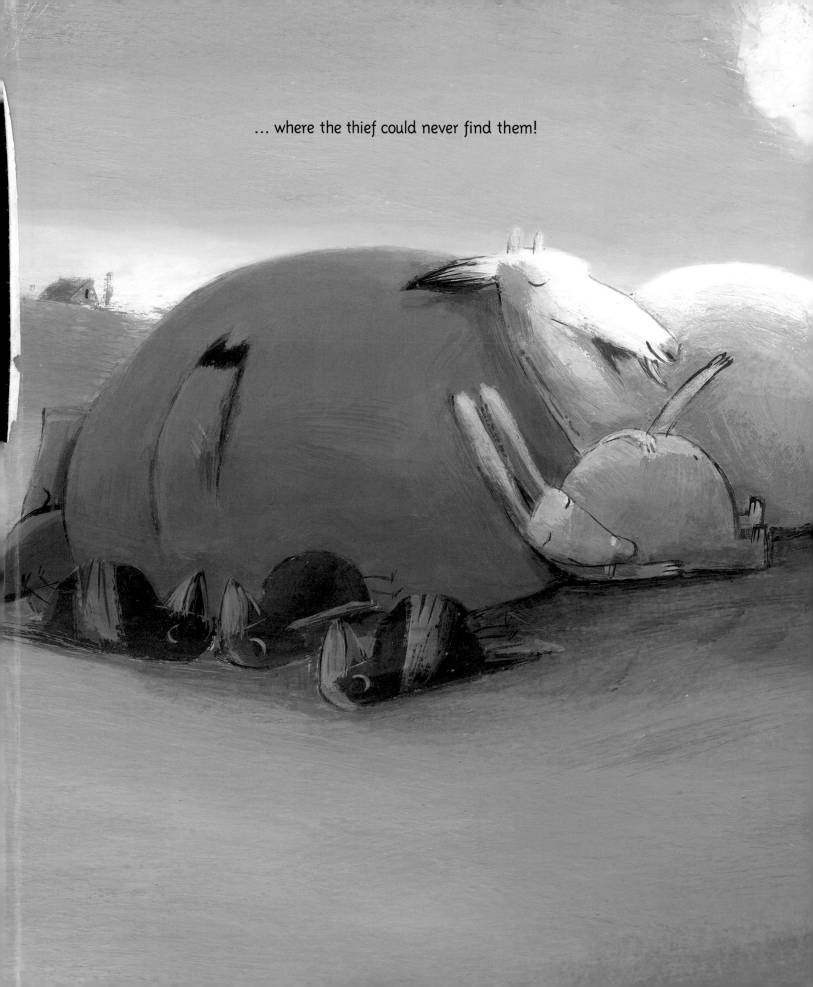

The End